MW00910692

SYLVESTER & TWEETY

READ THE MYSTERY

Curse of the Nile

Bath New York Singapore Hong Kong Cologne Delhi Melbourne

Story by Sid Jacobson
Pencils by Pablo Zamboni and Walter Carzon
Inks by Duendes del Sur
Color by Barry Grossman

First published by Parragon in 2008
Parragon
Queen Street House
4 Queen Street
Bath BA1 1HE, UK

Copyright © 2008 Warner Bros. Entertainment Inc.
LOONEY TUNES and all related characters and elements are trademarks
of and © Warner Bros. Entertainment Inc.
WB SHIELD: ™ & © Warner Bros. Entertainment Inc.
(s08)

PARR 8200

All rights reserved. No part of this publication may be reproduced,
stored in a retrieval system or transmitted, in any form or by any
means, electronic, mechanical, photocopying, recording or
otherwise, without the prior permission of the copyright holder.

ISBN 978-1-4075-2629-4

Printed in USA

For weeks, Granny had talked to Tweety and Sylvester about the great sights to be seen in the country of Egypt. Now, at last, they were there, and they would find more mystery in Egypt than they imagined.

It was certainly hot as they strolled along the bank of the Nile
to visit the **Mystical Pyramid**, a place overrun with strange tales.
"It's the home of one of the world's great puzzles," said Granny.

"Big deal. The only puzzle I want to solve is how to capture that canary," Sylvester thought.

"He'd better not twy anything," Tweety thought. "It's too hot to be worried about that puddy tat."

And things would get hotter!

"It's so big," gasped Granny, gazing at the pyramid.
"And so strange," said a man who suddenly
appeared at her side.

The man had a monocle in one eye and a sneering
look in both. He bowed and clicked his heels as he spoke.
   "It is a pleasure to meet you, madam," he said to Granny.
"I am the great detective Sherman Schmutz."

"I am here to solve the mystery of the curse of the Nile,"
he continued. "And to find the long missing Prince Ali Bari."

Seven years ago, the young prince went into the pyramid.

Before he disappeared, he uttered, "Just send someone to get me and I'll return." But the prince hadn't been seen since.

It was indeed a mystery.

"They believe that a curse is the only explanation for the missing prince," Schmutz explained. "Because I am such a great detective, they have hired me to find the prince and I will succeed!"

Tweety stared at the boastful man. "Bet I find the pwince before he does," said Tweety.

"Find the prince?" Sylvester spat out. "You couldn't find your own reflection in a mirror!"

"I can, too, Mr. Puddy Tat," said Tweety, and he flew
into the Mystical Pyramid, with Sylvester at his tail.

Inside the candlelit pyramid, Tweety scampered down one mysterious passageway after another, followed by Sylvester. "You'll never get out of here, you stupid bird," he called out to Tweety. "And I'll leave with a big smile on my face!"

The pyramid was filled with paths, many crossing each other and then ending at a sudden wall. "If that puddy tat ever caught me, I hate to think of what he'd do!" Tweety muttered as he once again came to a dead end.

"Shouldn't we follow them?" Granny asked Detective
Schmutz, outside the pyramid. "I don't like to leave them alone."
Schmutz shook his head. "If they cannot find the prince, how
can ve find a canary and a cat? Come, ve shall vait at the exit
on the other side."

Running through the pyramid, Tweety searched for a way out.
Though he found new paths leading him to other parts of the
pyramid, he never found the long lost Prince Ali Bari.
Almost a half hour later, Tweety ran into some big trouble!

With the force of a raging wind, Sylvester suddenly came running headlong at the canary.

"I've finally got you!" the cat snarled. His arms outstretched, his claws reaching for Tweety, Sylvester then jumped at the frightened bird. Tweety screamed and . . .

. . . Tweety ducked!

Sylvester jumped over the crouching bird and into the hard
wall behind him. SMASH! Sylvester fell in a heap on the ground.

Sylvester was knocked out by the crash and Tweety,
standing at his side, wondered what he should do.

"I can't weave him here," he said. "That would be too cwuel. He'd never find his way out." Tweety helped Sylvester up and started to walk with the dizzy cat along a route that he hoped would lead them out of the pyramid.

They found the exit, and met Granny and Detective Schmutz outside.

"See," said Schmutz, smiling. "Ve didn't have to vait long. Now I shall go inside the pyramid and solve this mystery," he said.

Looking around, Tweety suddenly knew where to find the prince. And it wasn't inside the Mystical Pyramid.

A short time later, Tweety returned, leading a man in a headdress and a very long beard. It was the long missing Prince Ali Bari!

"For seven years I've waited for someone to come to me," the prince said to Granny, Sylvester, and Detective Schmutz, who stood at the entrance to the Mystical Pyramid. "Finally, the canary came."

A party was held at the prince's palace.

"Only Tweety saw the SECOND pyramid!" said Granny to the crowd.

"Why doesn't she shut up?" muttered Sylvester.

"Vhy doesn't she be kviet?" said Detective Schmutz.

"Because she's my loving Granny," thought Tweety, as everyone cheered and applauded the great canary detective.